STAYING COOL

Joely Carey

STAYING COOL

Joely Carey

BARRON'S

First edition for the United States, its territories and dependencies,
and Canada published 2002 by Barron's Educational Series, Inc.

Conceived and created by
Axis Publishing Limited
8c Accommodation Road
London NW11 8ED
www.axispublishing.co.uk

Creative Director: Siân Keogh
Designer: Juliet Brown
Project Editor: Charlotte Stock
Production Manager: Sue Bayliss

NOTE

The opinions and advice expressed in this book are intended as a guide only. The publisher and author accept no responsibility for any injury or loss sustained as a result of using this book.

All inquiries should be addressed to:
Barron's Educational Series, Inc.
250 Wireless Boulevard
Hauppauge, New York 11788
http://www.barronseduc.com

Library of Congress Catalog Card No: 200109975

ISBN 0-7641-5564-4

9 8 7 6 5 4 3 2 1

Separated by United Graphics Pte Ltd
Printed and bound in Singapore by Star Standard Industries (Pte) Ltd

Contents

introduction 6

what is "cool?" 8

peer power 26

good to be bad? 40

inner cool 60

help is at hand 78

Introduction

Hi!

How are you? Good, I hope. This book was written to help guide you through the tricky teen years. Yes, it is a turbulent time but it should also be the best of times.

This Teen Talk guide is smart and outspoken, just like you. It won't answer every question, but it will guide you well. And it's not a substitute for family or friends either; just a starting point. Hopefully it will get you thinking, and making up your own mind, about how to stay cool.

Think of this book as a little guardian angel helping you to stay streetwise and true to yourself, your friends, and your family.

1

what is "cool?"

As a teen in today's society the pressure is on to think right, dress right, study right, do it all right. At the same time, we want to stay hip, smart, confident, and cope with puberty, boys, sex, drugs, everything. There'll be good and bad experiences, and we'll learn something from all of them.

Staying Cool

The perfect girl, with the perfect hair, skin, teeth, figure and, of course, the perfect life. She's a figment of some ad man's dream.

definitely not for sale

Do you conform or do you walk your own path? It's up to you. But individuality can't be bought. It's a sense of self that you were born with — don't let the commercial world rob you of that.

Where do a lot of designers get ideas for their fashion collections?

The street.

Where do musicians get their sounds?

The street.

You might not realize it but teens are the world's most wanted people. Advertisers, manufacturers, pop stars, designers, you name it, the whole world wants teens on their side. And they'll spend millions of dollars trying to convince us of that. Teens are hot property and everyone wants a piece of us. Keeping hold of our own identity can be tough when it seems that all society wants to do is to mold us.

And it's so tempting to let ourselves be led. Because the world of media hype is a clever one. From music to magazines the message is the same. Conformity. All they want to do is to get teens to buy into their world; to "brand" us. Why? Because as teens we are the consumers of tomorrow. If they can snare us now, they hope they've got us for life. How does it feel to be so wanted? A bit scary, eh?

decisions, decisions

If you thought this book was a lecture, think again. It's not. It's written to help you, and to give you the facts so you can make choices that are right for your situation. In some cases other teens have spoken about their experiences. You might find that their choices, good and bad, will inform and, sometimes, inspire you.

Consumerism, branding, and image are everywhere. And it can be tough to keep a sense of ourselves with all this going on. For a quick reality check just look at those around you—your friends, family, peers. Do they look like the plastic people on TV, billboards, and in magazines? Nope. Because they're real. Not fake images pretending to be our very best friends.

getting a grip

Keeping our heads when we're in the middle of all of this change is the tricky part. Knowing when to accept a challenge or to walk away. To stay streetwise we need to: understand other teens in difficulty and support them; keep safe as we tread the path of sexual discovery; and, most of all, stay informed enough to avoid the dangers of drink and drugs.

Friendships

When home is driving you crazy and school is on your back, you need friends.

Being a teen is complicated. We're on the road to adulthood, which is tough enough, but along the way we have to deal with puberty, peer pressure, school, boys, parents . . . the list just keeps going on and on.

look. this is me!

Sometimes we try be to someone we're not — smart, sexy, or outrageous — just to get friends. To find our true friends, all we need to be is ourself. If that isn't good enough for them, they're not worth it.

One of the ways to survive the teen obstacle course is through our friends. As a teen our friends are the center of our universe. Good friends are always there for us: they support us, give good advice, never judge us, and always steer us in the right direction.

In an ideal world those friendships will last unblemished forever, but we need to accept that as we grow and develop our individuality, so our friends will too. Sometimes we will go in the same direction; other times we will pull apart.

Usually we choose friends who mirror a part of our personality. It's only natural to be drawn to people who have similar tastes in music, clothes, and hobbies. But finding a good group of people isn't always easy; in fact making true friendships can be tricky. Just because they're our friends doesn't mean they're always good for us. People change and not always for the better. If someone is being a drain on us (check out the Toxic Test) then we need to tell her that we want a real friend.

toxic Test for selfish friends

TOXIC FRIENDS TAKE, TAKE, TAKE, BUT GIVE NOTHING BACK.

TELLTALE SIGNS OF A TOXIC FRIEND?

She never shares.
She dumps you when she gets a new boyfriend but expects you to pick up the pieces.
She never compliments you—but always copies you.
She asks you to lie for her.
Phone calls are only ever about her life—she never asks how you are.
If you've got a toxic friend, do her a favor: tell her to stop being selfish.

friends in need

What can you do when a friend needs your help but you don't know what to do? You can't drag words out of someone if she wants to keep her mouth firmly shut. Let her know you are always there for her, no matter what. Encourage her to open up to you, and reassure her that you won't be judgmental. Always listen, show an interest in what she's saying, and be sympathetic. Then all you can do is wait. If she is in danger—either at home or school—ask if she wants you to go with her to get help. Maybe having you alongside could give her the courage she needs.

Fitting In

No one wants to be the odd one out; we all want to be one of the gang.

We all worry about fitting in. We want to be part of the crowd —accepted and inconspicuous. But doesn't being inconspicuous mean we're invisible too? No one wants to be so much a part of the crowd that they fail to get noticed, do they? Or maybe they do . . .

Fitting in shouldn't be about blending in, but about feeling as though we belong, being part of something bigger than us. And if we don't feel as though we belong, then we feel lost, excluded, and lonely. Not a nice place to be.

Mary, 16

It's taken me years to learn to be my own person. I've had some tough times, been treated badly by friends, allowed it to happen. Not anymore. I know that I am equal in all aspects to other kids my age, and worth exactly the same as everyone else. You need to be able to grasp that idea, stand up for yourself, and declare your individuality. If so-called friends can't accept that, then they aren't your friends.

faking it

Stick a group of teens in a situation and each one of them will fake something. It's a kind of self-protection; we all do it. If we're unsure we put on an act of bravado; puff ourselves up to appear older, bolder, and more knowing. And it's all a con. Underneath we're all unsure; worried that we'll come across as nerds, weirdos . . . and very uncool. Trouble is once we've been caught and exposed, we really do look like a nerd, and a faker! So stick to being you, being confident, and enjoying your life.

It's all very well going on about being individual and confident in ourselves, but if we don't feel that we fit in with our school, our neighborhood, or even our family, then life becomes much more difficult than it should be. And teens don't need that extra pressure; we want to fit in and belong.

Make yourself comfortable

Fitting in means feeling comfortable, whatever the surroundings, without pretending to be someone we're not. Even if we get the "fake us" accepted, our real self is still an outsider.

live by your own rules

It would be great to have a guidebook "Three easy steps to fitting in . . ." but each girl is different, with different friends. So you write your own rule book.

Sticks and Stones

People, no matter what age, still struggle with who they really are and what they really want. Being a teen is no different.

People sometimes allow themselves to be victims of vicious criticism just because they want to fit in. But peer pressure of the wrong sort can influence us to make bad decisions and drag us down. Ultimately it can reduce our own feelings of self-worth and can tip us into depression.

telling tales

We all have to put up with name-calling: shit happens, as they say. Anyone who wears glasses, braces, or has pimples has been teased. But when does name-calling become an offense? Well, that's a tricky one. We can all expect a bit of ridiculing and name-calling. (Me? I was called "frog eyes" for about two years in high school. I didn't like it, but I ignored it until eventually, fewer and fewer people called me it.) No matter how innocent the name-calling might seem at first, if it upsets you, then you have the right to want it to stop. Tell an adult, parent, older sibling, or teacher what is happening. They won't laugh at you and you won't be called a snitch.

People can discriminate against us for loads of reasons. Maybe we're a different race or religion, come from a different neighborhood, or maybe we look a little different.

Whatever the reason, some teens will quickly latch on to whatever it is about us that makes us different, to discriminate against us. They feel it makes us an easy target. Someone they can use as a butt for jokes which they think makes them look better, and let's them feel better about themselves.

But is being different a bad thing? Far from it. It's what makes us unique. Maybe our friends don't realize their so-called gentle teasing is upsetting. None of us really like having fun poked at us; so just let your buddies know if you don't find that joke funny any more.

singled out for attention?

IF YOU ARE BEING DISCRIMINATED AGAINST, SPEAK OUT.

Tell others in your family or neighborhood. If you are being discriminated against because of your color, home background, or religion, it's likely someone close to you has already experienced it. There's nothing new about name-calling except that it's new to you. Always stay true to yourself—allowing the views of a minority of people to change the person you are would be a tragedy. Instead, talk it over with others who have lived through it. Not only can they give you tips on how to handle it, but they are living, breathing proof you can get through it.

born to be you

Bow to peer pressure and we lose our own identity. If we never listen to our inner voice, we never turn out to be the people we were born to be.

Clone-Zone Alert

Peer group pressure (PGP) is the hardest situation to handle. It is always so much easier to do and say what everyone else is doing and saying; or is it more like what they say you should be doing and saying?

pressure spots

Peer pressure is everywhere: advertising, fashion, television, music, sports, and education. It's a form of gentle persuasion or manipulation that steers you away from the person you are.

If someone suggests something to us that makes us feel uncomfortable, you can bet it's a form of peer pressure. We should be able to say "No" to whatever it is and walk away; but it's not always that simple. And it's not just a problem for teens: many adults too find it tough to stay true to themselves when faced with a group of their peers.

Shame to be the same

Sometimes we all have to take the peer culture on board, conform a little to fit in. But conforming too closely to the way our peers think is going to turn us into clones of them. Just imagine if we had a slumber party and all our friends wore the same clothes, and listened to the same CD over and over. Sounds dull? You betcha. It's one thing to wear the same sneakers as our friends but a whole different issue to conform so much that we wipe out our individuality. But to be honest, being a teen is like one big game of chicken, where our life becomes the traffic-packed highway and the hazards we have to dodge are drugs, stealing, smoking, sex, and violence. So tread carefully.

subtle pressure makes its mark

PGP isn't always physical: it can be the way other girls take one look at our sneakers and say "So last year." That's all it takes for us to feel like a complete fool. It's tough but not impossible to stand up to peer pressure. Ask yourself: "Do I really want to put myself at risk just because another kid thinks it's cool? Who says they're right and I'm wrong? Since when did they know all the rules?." We constantly question our parents, so why not treat our peers the same way?

dealing with PGP

There are three ways to deal with peer pressure.

1. Stand true to yourself: say that you swore never to bully, smoke, take drugs, or steal, and you won't break that promise to yourself.
2. Laugh your way out of it: make a joke or a wise-crack and shift the spotlight elsewhere. But this option doesn't make the problem of peer pressure go away, it just postpones it.
3. Walk away from the situation, and possibly, those peers. If you get caught stealing that lip gloss, will they take the rap too; admit they coaxed you to do it?

Clicking with a Clique

A clique is just a bunch of friends, right? Well, no, there's more to it. The Oxford English Dictionary calls it a small, exclusive set, faction, or gang, no less.

le chic clique

Some cliques demand high entry fees: members must wear this season's colors and designer labels only. Are you getting value for your money?

The main problem with cliques is that they are exclusive, so that means not everyone can be in one . . . which is automatically a bad thing. Cliques tend to fall into distinct categories—jocks, goths, preppies, etc.—but maybe the mystery surrounding cliques isn't so deep. It's just that we tend to be drawn toward people like us, who share the same interests.

not so unobtainable

MOVIES SUCH AS "CLUELESS" PROMOTE THE MYTH THAT CLIQUES ARE FOR THE BEAUTIFUL PEOPLE. You know the types: kids with money, designer clothes, fast cars, beautiful friends, and textbook-perfect parents. They're all mythical —no one's life is that perfect.

Losing your identity

Those people in a clique feel secure, confident, and part of something special. They're in with the in-crowd. But those who are excluded feel like outcasts, social misfits who aren't good enough.

This is wrong and ultimately extremely damaging to them. Everyone has their own views, tastes, and style, right? So, live and let live. Just because you and your clique have like minds, doesn't mean that you are the chosen few.

oh so right oh so wrong

Cliques can be destructive when all the members have to look "right," be seen with the "right" people, have the "right" opinion, and do the "right" thing. Often you can be in a clique and kid yourself that outsiders think you are popular and beautiful, when in fact the rest of your class thinks that you and your clique are nerds.

cliqued out

But what happens if your clique dumps you? Suddenly you're out of favor and on your own. You've not only lost the people you thought were your friends, but you can be dumped on by other kids because you were something they weren't. Sometimes the power of the clique lies in its ability to exclude another person. Or, maybe you are made fun of because you were in, now you're out. Whatever, it's no party and it's a miserable place to be. Use the experience to improve your self-confidence. Sure, that sounds tough, but be yourself and get involved in other activities, drama, music, or sports. Whatever you do, don't put yourself in exile for fear of meeting up with your ex-friends. If you do, you're letting them have the upper hand; you lose out. Don't let them win.

Pack Instincts

Once you're in a clique, keeping hold of your own identity is the real challenge.

get yourself in or get out

CLIQUES, BY DEFINITION, AREN'T ACCEPTING OF OTHERS.
It's a case of the haves and the have-nots because not all teens are cool enough to meet the standards of others. And that's where it can start: that very fine line between having a group of friends and being in the company of subtle bullies.

At times the clique itself can become more important than the people in it. That's when clique leaders become dictators, and when you're in one of these exclusive sets you too sense a feeling of power. After all, you have been accepted when others haven't; that fact alone can give you an inflated sense of yourself.

A clique can be extremely judgmental, not only of others, but of its own clique members too. How many of you have been subjected to three-way calling? You know, when a member calls and asks you questions about another clique member, who is silently listening on the other line? You're being tricked: maybe the silent member gets hurt by things you say. Who benefits? No one.

Where cliques become dangerous is when group mentality takes over for the individuals. The group itself becomes a living, breathing thing; instead of your being concerned about poor Madison because she looks upset and in need of some support from a friend, you worry how her appearance will reflect on the clique, and that people will judge you by her failings, looks, and situation. All very bad and an unhealthy way to treat fellow teens.

where does it get you?

Nowhere. Into some brainwashing actually. Your individuality gets lost and that can only lead to trouble.

Ali, 15

Perhaps because I was new at school, I was quickly accepted by a group of six girls. They were all pretty, funny, and smart and we had great times. Six months later, things went bad: girls grew jealous of the attention I got from boys. Rumors started and I ended up in a shouting match with one of my "friends" because she had been so mean about one of my little sister's friends.The rest of the clique took sides with her, and made it clear I was no longer part of their little club. I was hurt but there was no going back. Still, I felt vulnerable because other kids in my year didn't want to be my friend either. And why should they? I'd not been interested in them when I had my cool friends. It was a very lonely time, and some days I was really low. Eventually I was absorbed into new friendships. True ones, based on me as a person.

Friends V. Cliques

We all need best friends. And what's better than five or six best friends who all have our interests at heart and will be there for us come what may? Nothing at all.

time for a reality check

If you are in a clique:
Do you openly welcome others into your social circle?
Do you care for each other come what may?
Would you stand up for your beliefs regardless of what others in the clique thought?
If you answered "No" to any of these questions, it could be a sign your clique has become too self-important—sounds like it's centered on intolerance and power, instead of true friendship.

Not all experiences of cliques are bad. For some of us, having a group of like-minded friends that we know well and trust can be a big help. For others, if our family life is unsettled and difficult, having the support of a large clique can be the difference between making it through to adulthood and going off the rails. Of course, we tend to gel with other teens who like the same stuff as we do; dress like us, have similar personalities.

If your clique puts other people or cliques in your school/neighborhood down, then there is something more going on than just a group of friends hanging out together. Different schools have different types of cliques. For many teens high school is a difficult enough time without being obviously ostracized by cliques. Suddenly teens have to be seen to fit in; when they can't their self-esteem is shattered.

a whole lotta friends

There's nothing wrong with having a large group of friends as long as: friendships stay true; egos are abandoned; others are accepted regardless of their beliefs, looks, and social standing.

One-to-one friendships

Cliques are a fact of school life—some even survive through to graduation day—but best friends are our most important asset. They're the ones we share everything with and have a true relationship with. Instead of searching out a clique for stability, why not focus on the friendships you already have? If you don't want to do that, at least recognize that having a best friend is important too.

Katie, 15

I think it's fine to be in a clique: they're just your friends and make you feel loved and happy. Teens who don't like cliques must be confusing them with bullies or something. Today's teens aren't forming cliques to find exclusivity, but to be with people they can connect with.

2

peer power

Our peer group can be the best thing in our life or the worst. This usually depends on whether we are "in" or "out." This chapter helps us to handle peer groups and enjoy being in them, and out of them. It also explains that we don't need to be in a group to be a cool person.

Feeling Blue

Bad moods, low moods: they both mean the same and are part and parcel of life.

comfort zones & pamper nights

SOMETIMES WE NEED TO CHEER OURSELVES UP. TRY THESE.

Save parts of your childhood in a trinket box. Fill it with bits and pieces from your younger years; toys, books, photos. That way you'll always have special reminders of good memories to cheer you up. Have regular pamper nights in the bathroom. Deep condition your hair, apply a facial, do your nails, and listen to your fave sounds.

Who's having a bad mood day? At least half your friends probably, which is completely normal. As long as you don't go around barking at people and calling them names, just because you feel low. But hey, you're too cool for that sort of thing aren't you?

If you're always perky you're either (a) **incredibly lucky** or (b) **lying.** Accept that some days you've got more happy genes than others. Just don't make other people pay the price. If you feel low, and want to take some time out, go to your room or the school library. Chill out. Often a walk can perk you up. Being physically energized can boost your mental energy too.

For us girlies, bad moods and irritation are closely linked to hormonal changes leading up to, and through, puberty.

Then every month an onslaught of hormones can cause chemical imbalances making us moodier, snappier, and weepy, all rolled into one. Plus we have to cope with the transition of losing our childhood and moving into adulthood. That can be tough too; but it doesn't last long. We soon find our niche again.

fine—be moody

Having moods is normal. If you're worried about your moods, be open. Don't worry alone, you'll just feel worse.

signs of depression

- Do you struggle to get out of bed each morning?
- Do you feel you want to hide from the world?
- Are you crying a lot?
- Have you been lying?
- Are you more irritable?
- Do you have trouble sleeping?
- Have you lost interest in favorite hobbies?
- Have you lost contact with close friends?
- Do you ever think of hurting yourself?
- Do you feel your life is hopeless?
- Have you gained or lost lots of weight in a short time?

If you answered "Yes" to four or more of these questions, it might be time to visit your doctor or school counselor. Tell them your symptoms and let them help you to pinpoint what's getting you down.

Climbing Back Up

Low feelings show themselves in different ways. Even if it doesn't seem like you will ever feel better, you will.

Teenage depression is often a temporary thing. When the troubles of being a teen in today's society seem overwhelming, depression often sneaks in just to make you feel even worse. But you can share your problems. If you feel like hurting yourself you must seek help. Teens who injure themselves are crying out for help, but sometimes if you don't ask, no one will know. Most of all, don't hide yourself away, even if it seems impossible to ask for help; you must.

me, me, me me, me

We've all had times of soul-searching, feeling miserable and overly sensitive. Too much of anything is never good. In time, moodiness turns into selfishness. That's when we need to change paths.

Speak out

Pretending you are OK will make the situation worse. Although teens often feel like super heroes, there are times when they can't always make things right . . . and this is one of them. True, no one can snap their fingers to make you instantly better, but they can and will help you. Talk to a friend, your big brother or sister, or an older relative. If not, try your school counselor or doctor. If you can't ask for help outright, write a letter or a poem to a close friend or adult, asking them to drop by. A problem shared is a problem halved. It's an ancient saying but as true now as ever.

putting it into words

ONE WAY TO STEER YOURSELF OUT OF DEPRESSION IS TO KEEP A JOURNAL.

Writing down your thoughts, and feelings, and activities, and poetry can help get things out of your system. Plus, as time moves along you can read back and see how you came out of each difficult situation. Your own experiences act as a handbook for life. You read what you have lived through, your highs and lows, and see for yourself that you had the power within yourself to change your life path.

a friend in need

Teendom is a time when depression sometimes creeps in and hits us when we least expect it. As a friend you want to help.

DO:

- Let them know that no matter how big or small the problem is, they can talk to you about it
- Suggest things to do
- Allow them space to be alone

DON'T:

- Be too overbearing
- Give up at the first refusal
- Bear the burden of their depression alone

Suicide is not the way

There may be times when closing the door and never breathing again seems like the only way out, but it isn't.

talking for your life's worth

Deciding to take your life is the last decision you will ever make.
Call someone, anyone, and talk.

National Hopeline Network
1–800–SUICIDE
1–800–784–2433

Talk for all your life's worth and then listen to what they have to say. Problems that might seem never-ending to you can sometimes be resolved, or even lightened, by an outsider.

With the stress and strain of modern life more teens are suffering depression. Worse still, as many as 4,000 teens in the U.S. kill themselves every year. The reasons why they do it are endless. One thing for certain though is that suicide is a horribly permanent solution to a very temporary problem.

Often we can feel as though we want out of the world we live in. But that's no answer. What can be the cause of deep depression? You name it: stress, exam pressure, peer pressure, loneliness, insecurity, feeling out of control, feeling ugly, fear of never getting a partner. Yes, they are all heavy problems in their own right but every single one of them can be resolved. Help is out there for you.

Pass it by, then pass it on

It sounds like just another cliché but this one's 100 percent true. Surviving a situation where you have hit rock bottom and coming out at the other end a full person will make you an invaluable human being. Honestly. Because you will have so much strength to share with others. Sure, it might not seem so right now, but give yourself time to heal, to regain your strength and you can become one of life's true soul sisters. You'll be able to help and advise others trying to find a way to get along that same difficult path.

recognizing depression

You need to know how to recognize depression for the monster that it really is. But that's easy to say but harder to do because depression has many faces: it wants you all to itself, so that it can eat you up, destroy your ability, and demolish your soul. Don't let it. When you detect the slightest sign of depression in yourself, just do one thing. Share it. Ask for help and then beat it. Don't give up and don't let situations that are out of your control take control of you. Be strong enough to recognize that you need help, then be even stronger and ask for that help. Suicide isn't the answer. It's just the end.

Dealing with Death

When someone you know and love dies, you will feel all sorts of emotions.

No two ways about it—the pain of losing somebody will hurt. And it might make you depressed, or so angry that you'll want to lash out at everybody. How could life be so cruel as to take that person you loved so much away? And why? No one seems to know the answer, which just leaves you feeling empty and even more angry. Why bother with anything any more? It makes more sense to close off from the world, doesn't it?

leave it in the past

Don't blame anyone, and especially not yourself, for things that you have left unsaid or done. That belongs to the past and you need to look ahead now, so move on.

Or maybe you think it's better to act like nothing has happened, that being this near to death has taught you just one thing—that life is for living. So you party harder, neglect your schoolwork, perhaps experiment with drugs and alcohol. Why worry about the future, when you might die soon, right? Wrong. The only given in this life is that we're gonna die—a freaky thought, but true. And when a family member dies, it sometimes makes this all too real for us.

Attending a funeral might seem scary, but it is the perfect time to mourn the person you have lost. If you find it too tough to attend or you'd rather mourn privately, do it. Just remember to explain your reasons to the family. They'll understand.

celebrate the dead

Death is a tragic part of life and you will miss that person forever, but it doesn't mean you'll never be happy again. Your feelings for that loved one are still genuine and you should try and celebrate those emotions. Talk to whoever you can about how you are feeling; your friends, your famiiy, a school counselor, or youth club leader, anyone you trust enough to listen.

in memory of . . .

Your anger, depression, and disbelief are all part of the grieving process and it will take you some time before everything feels anything like normal again, but it will eventually. Use your creativity and imagination—yes, you do have the talent in you—to express your grief and/or your love for that person. You don't have to be an artist to write a song, a poem, or a letter that let's you "speak" to that person or express how you feel about them. Or why not paint a picture that captures your feelings? It will help you to make sense of what's happened and be a lasting tribute to that person. You don't have to show what you've made to anyone else, just file it away safely and look at it when you feel the need.

Bullying

Most of us will encounter bullying at some point in our lives. Although it is unpleasant, we can survive it.

A bully is someone who likes to intimidate us and make us feel inferior. It doesn't always have to be physical: teasing, spreading rumors, or stealing our stuff are types of bullying. We all know kids in school who are bullied and humiliated regularly. They are picked on by people who believe, for some unknown reason, that they are better than them, and that they have a right to dish out ridicule and physical punishment. They don't.

Sure it would be a lot easier if bullies weren't around, but they always have been. It's part of growing up. Sometimes bullies get off on the power they feel when their victim gives in to their demands. Other times, bullies like to show off, and make a display of their power to humiliate. If there were no cheering

how to tell your parents

JUST MAKE SURE THEY ARE PREPARED FOR THE NEWS

Explain that you are going to tell them something that they will feel strongly about, but that you don't want them to do anything that will make things worse for you. They love you and they will want to help you resolve a situation that is making you unhappy.

crowd, maybe the bullying would stop. It's important that we don't let ourselves be part of the energy that bullies need, so walk away.

adults have their uses

Sometimes we need adults to help us out. Some teens who are bullied become depressed and anxious. Don't let that happen to you.

If you are bullied

Being constantly picked on is a humiliating, depressing, endless cycle. You feel alone, screwed up, and at times suicidal. And who blames you? Understandably you are scared, but don't let your fear of the bully stop you from getting help. Remember you have a right to be happy—a right to be who you are—and the bully is taking that away from you.

beating the bully

There is rarely a knight in shining armor to solve your problems, so you usually have to make the changes yourself. No one is asking you to stand up to your aggressor and defy him or her, but you do have to be the person to make things start to happen. The first thing is to tell someone. Your parents are a good first stop. Sound like the worst thing you could do? It ain't. All schools have an anti-bullying policy, so if you can't talk to your folks try a school counselor. Help is at hand—just ask.

What Makes a Bully?

Often, the only way that bullies can deal with their anger is to make someone else feel as miserable as they do.

could you be a Bully?

Have you made someone else feel small, humiliated, made them purposely scared or upset? Next time, think: don't be a bully.

We all know a person who is different—the class loner or the kid with the quiet voice—every school year has one. And how many times do the supposedly cool kids make fun of this person? Once is too often. Just because these kids are different from us doesn't make them weird or odd. If we don't accept them for what they are, then we are just as guilty as the bully.

Bullies deserve happiness too

Bullying can be a cry for help. Often teens who are bullies have emotional problems themselves; maybe their home life is bad or they are being bullied or abused by others. Perhaps they themselves have low self-esteem. If you have been a bully, you're not a bad person, you deserve to be happy too. But making other people feel your pain isn't the way forward.

Ask yourself why you do the things you do. Then get someone to help you work through that. This can be through a school counselor or an adult you trust. If you have bullied others, you have to change. Accept people's differences.

what do you do if you see bullying?

YOU WANT TO HELP, FINE. BUT DON'T PUT YOURSELF AT RISK
Make sure you've read the situation correctly. Then take action. Tell a counselor or teacher. You don't have to accuse anyone of anything. Simply telling the truth could be enough to set wheels in motion.

Jo, 18

I wasn't beaten up, but I was picked on, teased, and ridiculed. Why? I lived in a small town, went to a different school, had weird eyes, wore strange jackets, oh, and I hadn't had a real boyfriend. I was just 14. Things came to a head one semester, when some kids blocked my way in the alley. I could have turned back, but I'd armed myself with lines that I'd been rehearsing for when this moment arrived. When the taunts started, I answered back: "My eyes, clothes and school aren't weird, just different from yours." Line No. 1 delivered. Deep breath in, then "And I haven't got a boyfriend from around here because you're all dorks. Who'd date a dork?" Silence. Then one girl started to laugh. "She's right. You are dorks. All of you." Suddenly, I was "in," but I never became close to any of them. My real friends were the girls who accepted who I was.

3

good to be bad

The teen years are often the time for us to rebel. To fight back against all the rules and regulations laid down by our parents and society. We can feel powerful, emotional, and in need of making a stand. We want to experiment, experience new things. Great. Do it. Just as long as we don't forget that we have to live with the choices we make; and remember that every choice has a consequence, so we need to think hard before we leap.

Dying for a Smoke

Smoking: so sexual, provocative, seductive, and oh so deadly.

Smoking is the largest preventable cause of premature death and disability in the United States. It kills 400,000 Americans every year and makes hundreds of thousands of others ill. It's not just those who smoke, but people who inhale second-hand smoke, the passive smokers, that suffer.

frazzled fingertips

Ever seen the mustard-yellow skin of a smoker's fingers? Hardly a beauty must-have is it?

A staggering 90 percent of adults who smoke want to quit, but fewer than 10 percent of those who try actually stub out for good. This shows just how addictive the nicotine is in cigarettes. Smokers know it's killing them, but they still can't give it up. In fact, the nicotine in cigarettes is extremely powerful and an addiction to the stuff is as strong as that caused by heroin and cocaine. Some studies have even shown that smoking can be linked to teen depression. You don't have to be Ms. Brainbox to figure out that smoking is bad for you. Period.

Most adults who smoke are trying to quit. They started thinking it was cool. Now they can't give it up. Nicotine is a drug; a deadly addictive drug. Don't start and you never have to go through the agony of stopping, or dying of incurable cancer. Let's not forget that. If you need more insight, just visit your local pediatric cancer department. Those kids are dying of a cancer they haven't asked for. Think they'd like a cigarette? Dumb question? You got it.

looks so cool doesn't it?

All those actresses in films. Being seductive, independent, feisty, grown up... That slim white stick that you hold at the corner of your mouth—inhale its smoke, then lick your lips and exhale—is a killer. Each drag of a cigarette brings you closer to illness, disease, and death. Plus teens using nicotine and alcohol are more likely to try out other harmful chemical drugs. Be smart and stop before you even get started.

want to look older?

Smoking might look good, but is it really? It makes your breath stink, stains your teeth, and chokes your chest. It causes deadly serious illnesses: lung cancer, heart disease, emphysema, respiratory problems, and vascular disease. It also ages your skin terribly—quicker than you can say 20 Marlboro Lites. No amount of wonder creams can turn back the clock on years of nicotine abuse. You get fine lines around your mouth and exaggerated crow's feet by your eyes. In your teens that seems an age away, but at 30 you shouldn't feel or look old. But a smoker will. She'll have wrinkles where her nonsmoking friends are still fresh-faced and could pass for ten years younger than her.

Resisting the Weed

Knowing the downsides of smoking is one thing, but refusing a cigarette in front of Ms. Cool of the School herself is another.

Ooh, what do you do? Take it? Refuse? C'mon, refuse the coolest girl in the school? Are you kidding? No kidding. You could take it. Have a few puffs, cough your guts up, look like a real nerd as you do so, and then have her (and her adoring crowd) smile pityingly at you for being so hopeless at smoking. Or you say you don't smoke; tried it but don't like it. Sorry. Then add, "You know it kills almost half a million Americans

Sarah, 17

My Dad looks really awful: gray, lifeless, and old, but he's only 38. He's dying of lung cancer because he has smoked since he was a teen. In every photo, he's got a cigarette in his hand or mouth. Those white sticks have robbed him of his health, and soon they'll rob me of my father. I wish I could turn the clock back, stop him from ever having that first puff, but I can't. I just have to enjoy what time we have left as a family. But I am so angry with him. You wouldn't drink poison, knowing it could kill you. So why smoke? It's just as stupid.

Bettie, 17

A year ago, I started dating a really cute guy. He asked me out and we went to the movies. He was sweet and *soo* sexy. On our third date I lit a cig. His face was a picture . . . of disapproval. That night he cut short our kiss, saying "I can't—your mouth tastes disgusting" How dare he? I stormed home. The next day he dumped me—by text. And I'd thought smoking was cool.

a year, every year? Crazy isn't it?." At that point you switch the conversation to her favorite subject—her. If she keeps offering you a cigarette, ask her what's cool about cancer? It kills you. She might say, "Yeah, who's to say you won't get knocked over by a bus crossing the road?." The answer to that is "Maybe, but if I saw a bus hurtling toward me, would I step in front of it? No." The question's answered, with plus points on your side. If Ms. Coolpants and her followers can't accept that not everyone thinks like them, their friendship ain't worth it. And who's to say she's more streetwise than you? Smoking isn't cool. It's dumb. People do it because they can, because they think it's grown up, and it's a way of going against what we have been told to do. Find other ways to rebel, ways that won't damage your health.

Big, Bad Booze

Alcohol is rarely referred to as a drug, but it is, and a very addictive one too.

Luscious but loaded

Wine coolers look like juice sparklers but they have just as much alcohol as a 12-oz. beer.

According to the law, you must be over 21 to drink or possess alcohol. But it is an accepted fact that most teens will experiment with alcohol way before then. Drinking might seem glamorous, but in reality it isn't. Although it isn't viewed with the same contempt as other drugs, booze is just as addictive as nicotine and just as deadly.

Teens' bodies are still developing, so alcohol has a greater impact on your physical and mental well-being.

Sam, 17

When I was 16, I went to baby-sit with some friends. The family had a large liquor cabinet and my friends dared me to drink a slug out of each bottle. Stupidly, I did. I was blind drunk and felt out of control. My friends panicked and sent me home in a cab. That night I vomited so badly my mom took me to the emergency room. I felt stupid for abusing my parents' trust in me and was grounded for three months.

Slang names include booze, sauce, hooch, juice, and brewskis—whatever you call it, the end result is still the same.

Alcohol is glamorized in advertising, movies, and on TV. Yes, in the right circumstances it can be pleasant, but only ever in moderation, and only ever when you stay firmly in control. How glamorous is it to be staggering out of a party only to throw up all over your new shoes by the back door? Umm, not very.

Being a strong person will help you when faced with the big question: to get drunk or not. It's not just your drinking that's a problem, but if your friends are drinking to excess too. Their inability to control themselves can result in dragging you into awkward situations. Be a true friend to them and help them say no too.

how much is too much?

If you start drinking before you are 15, you are four times more at risk from alcoholism than those who begin when they are 21 or over.

- Alcohol is the most abused substances in the United States
- Alcohol damages just about every organ in your body
- Drinking can cause memory loss, impaired reflexes, and poor coordination
- Drinking to excess can cause vomiting, diarrhea, blackouts, coma, and even death.
- Alcohol mixed with medication can also be extremely dangerous

One drink can make you fail a breath test. In some states, drivers under the age of 21 found to have any alcohol in their system can lose their driver's license, be heavily fined, or have their car permanently taken away.

Out of Control

Some people drink with the impression that they will be more confident. That's a myth.

letting drink talk for you

Drinking doesn't make you fit in. It makes you cross boundaries that you wouldn't dare to breach when sober.

Over-indulging in alcohol is extremely dangerous. Alcohol doesn't make you more confident, it just lowers your inhibitions. Whereas sober you would think kissing your brother's best friend would be nice, but unlikely, a few alcopops later and you're eating his face in a very undignified manner. When you remember, you'll cringe with embarrassment. No one's saying when you're drunk you lose your morals, but you're not in full control, which leads to situations that put you at risk.

Carrie, 16

At a summer school party I got drunk and started dancing with an older boy I liked. We started kissing, then he led me off on my own. I was drunk and my defenses were down, so when he started touching me I let it happen. He left me alone with my clothes hanging off and went back to his friends laughing. They thought I was easy. I got called names for months afterward.

the aftermath of alcohol

Alcohol affects each person differently: for instance, women's bodies react more quickly than men's bodies to alcohol. It is carried through the bloodstream to the brain, stomach, internal organs, liver, kidneys, and muscles and stays in the body for several hours. Overdose occurs in young drinkers because they try to drink too much, too fast. This can lead to alcoholic poisoning; you can pass out, choke on your own vomit and die. Alcohol also brings out an aggressive side in you, so you end up arguing, fighting even. How cool is that?

Picture this: you're at a party where there's a really cool guy you like. You end up with him in a bedroom and he's getting hot and heavy. Before you know it, the situation has gone way too far. He gropes you, maybe you have sex. Were you with it enough to use a condom? No? Could you be pregnant? Yes. Could you have a sexually transmitted disease? Yep. And what about the stories that are bound to race around school?

ways to say "no thanks"

"I'M NOT INTERESTED"
"IT MAKES ME ILL"
"I DON'T DRINK"

Be prepared for a bit of a backlash. You're being sensible, not prudish. You're wised up about the whole drinking thing. In the morning when they look awful and feel even worse, you'll be fine. You're looking after yourself.

Doing Drugs

Taking drugs, any drug, won't magically make you popular, cool, or more attractive. It just numbs you, putting a hold on reality for a little while.

why do drugs?

Teens do drugs for various reasons:
To escape unhappy situations.
To compensate stress and pressure.
To gain street cred.

Okay, we all know drugs aren't good for us. But that doesn't stop us from being pressured or curious about trying them. Not so long ago, 14.8 million Americans aged 12 and over were using illegal drugs. Of those, 3.5 million were drug dependent.

Take a look at marijuana; also known as ganga, dope, weed, skunk, and grass. Whatever the name, it's a drug. A dangerous drug that affects our brains, and weakens our self-control. Why? Because there are 400 chemicals in marijuana—even more when it is heated and smoked. Some people claim this is a safe drug, a happy drug. No drug is safe. Drugs alter our normal state. Automatically, the one thing that we prize so much, our self control, is gone. We're no longer controlling the situation, the drug is controlling us.

Studies have shown that almost 50 percent of teens try dope before graduating from high school. And other research has shown dope is often a gateway drug, one that leads to using and experimenting with other drugs. That in itself is dangerous.

smoke gets in your head

KIDS AT SCHOOL WILL CLAIM EVERYBODY'S DOIN' IT.

They're not. If you were insecure, unsure, even unpopular before you smoked dope, you can bet you'll stay all of those things with a dose of paranoia thrown in. Smoking dope can make you very unstable, unpredictable, and dangerous to be around. Wouldn't you rather be in control and happy?

marijuana-the facts

To make up your own mind, you need the facts. Marijuana causes: brain dysfunction, lack of coordination, memory loss, paranoia, fear, panic, and anxiety. It can speed up the heart rate to 160 beats per minute, compared with a regular 70 beats per minute. It causes dilated blood vessels, making the whites of the eyes turn pinky. Panic feelings may be accompanied by sweating, dry mouth, and having trouble breathing. Hardly a recipe for a wicked night out is it? Plus this drug can exert power over your emotions, making you feel heightened sensations. Some people claim it just makes you really giggly. For others it causes deep paranoia; fear of the situation they're in and even of the friends around them.

The Usual Suspects

Here are the facts; the decision is yours. Is it ever worth the risk?

Meth Also known as crystal meth, ice, chalk, glass, crank, speed, it causes incredible euphoria, and increased alertness and sexuality. But when the drug wears off you crash, big time. The chemical imbalances caused in the brain result in hallucinations, extreme paranoia, violent behavior, weight loss, skin welts, suicidal tendencies, and severe depression. Not such a high after all.

Cocaine/crack Extremely addictive, cocaine can erode your nasal passages, leading to complete loss of the septum—the gristle that separates your nostrils. And each snort of cocaine puts extra stress on your heart.

Heroin The most lethal and destructive, this street drug changes the way nerve cells work in the brain. The cells get so used to having heroin around that they need it just to work normally. Users tend to inject it and risk HIV through sharing needles.

Club drugs These chemical drugs are highly dangerous and, if mixed with alcohol, become even more lethal. Ecstasy, or X, is taken to improve your mood and boost energy at all-night raves. Prolonged and chronic X abuse damages the brain, preventing normal thought processes.

GHB (Gammahydroxybutyrate), G or Georgia Home Boy: Low doses act as relaxants, but increased doses can result in ultra-sedative effects, coma, and death.

Rohypnol or roche is used as a date-rape drug because it is tasteless and odorless. It causes memory loss, drowsiness, low blood pressure, and confusion.

Ketamine or Special K can cause loss of memory to the point of amnesia, high blood pressure, delirium, and severe breathing problems.

LSD or acid causes unpredictable behavior, dependent on the user's personality. It can cause numbness, weakness, nausea, increased heart rate, sweating, lack of appetite, flashbacks, and sleeplessness.

Fun-Loving Criminals

The only way to deal with crime is to walk away. Nothing good can come of it.

the price of crime

There's no such thing as making a quick buck through crime. Commit a crime and you throw away your dignity, risk prison, and get a criminal record.

As teens, we're often pushing at boundaries as we flex our developing selves. Some of us get intrigued by authority, challenging it, and in some cases committing crime. This is a crazy path to tread. Not only can it get us in major trouble, it will do nothing for our self-respect.

Friends and associates might try to convince you to commit petty crimes: take clothing, cosmetics, or CDs. When there's a crowd playing dare, it can be hard to walk away, but

Sharon, 17

My friends and I met some girls from our school at the mall. They'd been stealing clothes and were on a high. They asked me to be a look-out in the next store and to try to distract staff if they were spotted. I was scared to do it and scared of being caught. I lied that I had to get home and they laughed at me, calling me chicken. But I didn't care 'cos I wasn't getting mixed up in all that.

Marcia, 15

"We were each dared to steal some makeup. At the store, I took an eye pencil but, as I walked away, a bell went off. I ran out with my heart pounding. I hadn't been caught, but I'll never forget how scared I felt; stupid too.

that's just what you have to do. If you find it tough, don't go to the mall. If you're not there, you can't be involved. Maybe you won't get caught; but if you do, your parents will be told, possibly your school, and you'll end up with a criminal record. The implications are huge. Don't even go there. Walk away.

Life on mean street

You might think that violence and shootings give gang life an exciting, if dangerous, edge. Now think of the down side: gang members are forever watching over their shoulders and can trust no one. If you want solidarity, respect, and friends for life, steer clear of the street gangs.

who wants to be roadkill?

Driving gives you independence. But if you drive a car without care, attention, and thought, you may as well go around brandishing a weapon. Because that is what your car has become. And there's no point in being a careful driver, if you get into a car whose driver has been drinking or taking drugs—they are incapable of safe driving. Look after yourself. Take a cab, bus, the subway, or call home for a ride.

Sex Games

For such a small word, sex has enormous significance. It's everywhere.

sex rules . the basics
Feel comfortable with what you're doing. Never be pressured into having sex. Always practice safe sexual activity.

Sex surrounds us, but guess what? It's still viewed almost as a taboo subject. Sometimes it feels like society is saying if we don't talk to teens about sex, they won't do it.

Yeah, right.

Quite a lot of teens are supposedly staying virgins longer, but many are still being sexually active and ignorant about it. Oral and anal sex have become the "norm" but it seems that a whole load of us don't think of these activities as "sex." So, for the record . . . sex includes oral, anal, vaginal sex, and masturbation. It's all sexual behavior and needs to be treated appropriately. With sexual images wherever we look, it's no wonder the messages get confused: don't have sex, but carry on being sexual.

Sex is often used as a form of rebellion; trouble is, sex isn't about getting noticed. It's a complicated relationship issue, and a major step toward adulthood. Done at the wrong time, with the wrong person, transforms it from being a warm, beautiful experience to a catastrophic one. Look at all the supposedly wised-up adults who still can't get their own sexual relationships right. Take the wrong steps toward sex and we can end up feeling hurt, cheap, and insecure.

choosing between boys and girls

Being unsure about your sexuality is common. And it's normal to have crushes on someone of the same sex; it doesn't mean you are gay. Give yourself time, relax, and let your true inner feelings guide you. Fretting about it only makes you anxious, unsure, and miserable. Call the National Hotline for Gay, Lesbian, Bisexual, and Transgender Youth 1–800–347–TEEN

sexual awakenings

What are the physical signs of sexual awakenings? First, your hormones start going crazy. Puberty usually kicks in any time after you reach nine years old. From then on you are under siege from these naturally occurring substances that take over your body, mind, and soul. Then you have incredible mood swings, breasts, pubic hair, sexual urges, crushes, erotic dreams, and a degree of uncertainty about this emerging new you. All very normal, but all very confusing.

When your first period arrives, it's the long-awaited sign that womanhood is just around the corner. But you can be a woman without having had sex. Because as all informed teens know, having sex does not a woman make.

Getting it Together

Boys want sex, and we want boys. But the two don't have to go hand in hand.

sex and fulfillment

Sex isn't something to be scared of, but without mutual respect, it is a cold, unfeeling act that leaves both parties unfulfilled.

Boys are under tremendous pressure to have sex when maybe they're not ready either. So don't let either of you get carried away with what everyone else thinks you should be doing. Sex is not about age, it's about emotional

Shona, 17

One of my friends kept on about how she loved sex, and that she was such a woman. It made me feel that I should be doing it too, so I had sex with my boyfriend. It was awful: rushed, fumbled, scary, and I felt cheap afterward. When I told her that I had done it too, she asked me what it was like. I smiled nervously and said, "You know, you've done it, plenty of times . . ." She glanced at the floor. "Actually I haven't, I've always been too scared." I was devastated. I'd lost my virginity because I'd wanted to fit in. My boyfriend told everyone I was a crap lay, and I felt used, cheap, and most of all stupid. Because it had been my choice, my decision, and boy was it the wrong one.

Gaby, 16

At 14, everything about sex excited me. I explored sexual activity with boys, touching, masturbating, oral sex, and I had penetrative sex at 15. Within six months I had three sexual partners.I was confusing sex with love;letting boys have sex with me thinking it was a fast track to love. It wasn't. They didn't love or respect me. In the end, I had no self-respect.

strength, maturity, and the depth of feeling in a relationship. Only you can decide when or how to have sex.

Sexual pressure is constant. Still, the rules to stick with, no matter what, are: look after yourself; be true to yourself; and never let anyone take advantage of you or your sexuality. Never enter into any kind of sexual act without being sure it is what you want. And make 100 percent sure that you are protected from disease and pregnancy. If you feel pressured into sex, walk away. Don't let a boyfriend or girlfriend put you in a position where you feel you must have sex.

keep on talking: sex can wait

ANXIOIUS TO FIT IN, BUT NOT SURE WHETHER TO GO FOR IT, HANG BACK, OR RUN AND HIDE?

Don't do any of the above; talk about it instead. With a school counselor, your parents (don't cringe — they've been there and have survived their teen years), an older relative, or a friend.

4

inner "cool"

Looking good and keeping healthy are only part of staying cool. To be smart and safe we need to be as chilled on the inside as we are on the outside.

Keeping our inner self strong and safe is the toughest job of all. Just remember that we can do it: all we have to be is strong and true to ourselves in times of struggle.

House Rules

Prove to our folks that we are mature and sensible and home life can become a chilled-out zone (well, nearly!).

If we want more privileges at home then we need to show our parents or guardians that we are able to take them on board and act responsibly.

Respect is a mutual concept. If we want respect from our folks, respect them back. The key rule is: always keep your promises. We know how jacked off we feel when friends let us down. That's how others feel when we do the same to them.

protecting their baby

Boys: accept that your folks aren't going to fall over themselves to welcome boyfriends into the family at first. After all you're "their little girl" and a boyfriend is one of the signs that you're growing up.

But she's my friend

Some friends will be welcome in the house, others won't be. Sometimes your family doesn't see the qualities in your friends that you do. The best way to ride this storm out is not to push the friends they don't approve of into their faces too much. Also ask yourself if there is a good reason why. Does your friend smoke, do drugs, or have bad grades? Often if your folks don't like a friend, it could be because they are worried they could be a bad influence. Tackle this head on. Tell them you know they don't like x, y, or z about your friend, but that you aren't going to behave that way. Once you've shown them you don't think that kind of behavior is cool, they should accept the friendship.

work it out at home

School: if you are having problems, let your family know. If they can, they will try to help.

. . . And if you want to fill your bedroom with friends, just run the idea past your Mom first. Being confronted with ten girls when she planned to have friends for dinner can be a shock.

Claiming your territory

Explain to your family that you need privacy. They have theirs and it's only right you have yours. They need to understand that your room is where you keep your life and that it is your private space. They should be fine with that, as long as you agree to keep it relatively tidy and free from plates of moldy food!

time to go home

Coming home time: stick to the agreed time and if you are going to be late, call. It doesn't take long and it saves the fights and mistrust.

The Folks at Home

Parents or guardians: good or bad we've all got them, but handling them can be tough.

Sure, our parents or guardians just want what's best for us, but often their concern makes us feel caged in, rebellious, frustrated, and confused. The life we lead and decisions we have to make are probably very different from the experiences of their generation. So whenever they make a decision we feel is unfair or which we don't understand, ask them to explain. Stop talking and it all goes downhill very quickly.

moms and daughters

"My Mom's always got along really well with my friends. But it reached the point where she tried too hard. I didn't want her to be my friend, I needed her to be my Mom." Tyler, 15.

"I usually confide in an older female cousin. My Mom would be upset if she knew but she's just a stranger to my world." Shannon, 14.

"My Mom's always been really open with me; I can tell her pretty much anything. She never judges me, and I feel she trusts me to make good decisions about important matters." Jo, 16.

understanding parents

what they say	what they mean
You can't wear that much makeup...	I'm worried people will think you're older than you are
That guy is no good for you	I don't want you getting hurt
I don't have time for this/Ask your Mom/Dad	I feel uncomfortable talking about this
Are you two serious?	Are you having sex?
Go tidy your room	I'm not your slave
You drive me crazy	I love you

Dear old Dad

When your Dad sees his little girl growing up, he might not know how to act around you. If it seems your Dad has become distant, take the lead and bridge that gap. Ask him to the movies, or do something you always shared together. Let him know you still want that father/daughter bond.

when parents turn bad

Sometimes parents abuse their children, verbally, mentally, physically, or sexually. If you are being abused, remember that you didn't ever deserve it and it's not your fault.

NO ONE WILL BLAME YOU.

Even if the abuse suddenly stops, you need help. It will take a lot of courage, but you have to do it. If you have a school counselor, go to them first. If not, call Childhelp USA at 1–800–4–a–child.

Family Divides

It is quite normal for a family's setup to change: pledging to be with one person for the rest of your life doesn't always work out.

Jessie, 17

My Mom died when I was a kid so it's just been me and Dad ever since. I'd be lying if I said our relationship is always cool, it's not. But we have managed to work out a good system where we talk and iron out problems between us.

If your Mom or Dad has left the family home, you are bound to be hurt, confused, and curious. Often a family splits up because one of your parents has been unfaithful to the other, or sometimes, as often happens in adult relationships they have just grown apart. Whatever the reason, just because your parents don't love each other anymore doesn't mean they don't love you. It's completely normal to feel a bit lost when your parents break up. Don't bottle it up; if you can, talk about your worries to an adult you can trust, perhaps a school counselor or teacher. Get your emotions out; bottled-up fears and anxieties can only be destructive.

Stepparents

If Mom or Dad remarries, you might feel that the "new" person thinks they have a right to discipline you, or is trying to take the place of the absent parent. Make sure you talk things through with your parent, alone. If you explain why you are worried, scared or upset, then they have a better chance of sorting it all out. Keeping quiet won't help anyone—least of all you.

coming together

There can be pressure to be a "perfect family," but it takes time to get to know one another. Relax, let it happen, and keep talking things over.

step siblings

If your parents remarry you can end up with an instant extended family. New people in your family setup are bound to create some differences, but remember that their lives have been turned upside down just like yours. If anyone understands how you feel, it's probably them; so when the time feels right, talk about how you are both coping. You could end up being a real help to each other. To make sure you stay friends, set out boundaries. Make sure you first tell them of any problems, and if they don't improve beyond that, tell your parent. If having a step sibling isn't all smooth sailing, don't be surprised or disappointed: complicated situations like these do take time to be resolved.

Self-Esteem

Low self-esteem can make people, teens especially, feel worthless. Which we are definitely not.

What is it? Well, self-esteem is how much you like yourself and value yourself as a person. It's no more complicated than that. Low self-esteem (LSE) is something we all suffer from to one extent or another. Usually LSE is caused by the way we have been raised. Perhaps we were surrounded by negativity, led to believe we were worthless, unable to achieve, and an all-around loser. Or perhaps our LSE has been

Amy, 19

LSE was invented for me. When my Mom died, it drove a wedge between me and my father. He took little interest in me, never gave me praise and as a result I felt worthless. I could have so easily become a nobody, flunked high school, and got a dead-end job. But I didn't. I spent hours reading in the library, mainly to get away. I made friends, achieved, let myself be happy and feel valued. But no one made it happen for me, I had to find my way there myself. And I'm so glad I did.

ways out of LSE

Unchecked LSE can be a trigger for violence, depression, suicidal feelings, drink, and drug abuse. Don't suffer in silence. Try to pinpoint where your feelings of LSE come from. Then, talk to a good friend or family member—they understand you best. If this isn't possible talk to a school counselor. They can get you the right counseling to let you believe in yourself so you can become a truly amazing young adult. Sounds impossible? It's not.

brought about by social circumstances and our peers. It is very common to have LSE at some point in our life, and it is perfectly sort-out-able.

Before we start labeling ourselves, or becoming victims—"Hey it's not my fault . . . I've got low self-esteem!"—let's remember that sometimes we can experience these feelings as regular teens finding our way through teendom. As a rule, teen anxieties will lighten and lessen as time goes by. But if we find these emotions getting more ingrained and restricting, it's likely we need to address them more seriously.

Is this you or is it LSE?

Put yourself down?
Demean your own abilities?
Feel generally anxious?
Go on the defensive quickly?
Feel that others do not value you or your friendship?
Lack faith in your judgment?

Confidence Tricks

Being confident is one of the keys to being truly happy with who you are. And our confidence will draw others to us.

feel good stay true

We need to be confident about ourselves ... to be confident we have to feel good about ourselves and to feel good about ourselves we need to be true to ourselves. Got it?

Confidence can be the difference between success and failure. And we've all got the ability to be confident, given the right environment and enough belief in self. We like to be with people who get parties started and are fun to be around. Why not take a page out of their book? Confidence lifts them and makes them more sociable. Let it do the same for you.

Sounds so simple, but it isn't. We're in the transition from child to adult. Not only do we have to grow up mentally, but just to add to our confusion, our bodies are changing too. Caught up in a web of hormone surges, physical changes, anxiety, and the fear of the unknown, it can feel easier to hide away from it all, retreat into ourselves. But hiding from the world makes it more difficult to come out again. Take quiet time away to think, but don't turn your back.

Don't knock it

Friends can make or break your confidence. Anyone who knocks your confidence should be an immediate ex-friend. True friends don't make their buddies feel inadequate; you act as each other's support systems. When one fails and lacks energy, the other kicks in, and boosts them up until they are as strong as before. Confidence is about knowing your good points and pushing them to the front. Don't compare yourself to others – you're you. Unique and individual.

confidence tricks

Walk tall. Hold your head high, and glide into any room. Your legs might feel like jelly but you look like Miss Confidence herself.

Sound confident. Yawn and stretch your vocal cords to prevent faltering. Practice talking in a clear, confident voice. Keep your head and chin up and make eye contact.

S M I L E. A simple, heartfelt smile makes all the difference–but no cheesy fake grins.

Be brave. Never let others put you down if you fail–at least you had the guts to try.

Be yourself. Why imitate? Only you can be you.

Mind Games

At times our feelings, both good and bad, can overwhelm us. But guess what? That's fine. Best of all, that's normal!

Just as our bodies change when we're teens, so do our minds. We are capable of extreme feelings, deep thoughts, philosophies, sadness, elation, and confusion. The depth of our emotions can be frightening. One of the things that marks us humans from our animal ancestors is our emotional strengths, our feelings, and our expressions. And sudden outbursts of emotion and feeling make us who we are. We shouldn't try to squash our strength of feeling or emotion about something, and need never be embarrassed by it.

Make a Show of it

Many celebrities say that in real life they are insecure and shy, but on stage and screen their passion for what they do takes over and it seems they could take on the world. So be positive about yourself.

Speak up

It's true sometimes that there is a time and place for strong feelings to be made known. We wouldn't want to start letting off steam in the middle of a history class; but if we feel strongly about certain issues, why hide it? Who is to say the views of others are more valid than ours? True, someone older can have a wider life experience and knowledge than us. But when it comes to feelings, no one has the upper hand. Everyone's feelings are important, valid, and should be heard.

getting ourselves worked up

As teens we like to get passionate about causes. We feel we can take on the world and win. And we can. Often we feel driven to speak out about great injustices: poverty, racism, discrimination, animal welfare . . . the list is endless. Getting involved can be very empowering too: as one voice, a group of us can make ourselves heard. It's also a window to our inner selves. We learn more about what makes us the people we are.

beware: badge wearer

Sometimes we might feel the need to get involved with a group just for the hell of it. Bad move. Jumping on a cause bandwagon to try to improve your popularity is not the right motivation. It won't make you less insecure—it might even make you more so, because you're with people who don't know the real you because you're faking it. Get it?
Good, So get real. Don't get involved with any group just because you hope it might help you jump up a notch or two in the eyes of your peers/family. Ditto if you want to join the "Make Crack Legal" brigade. Who are you trying to shock? And, more importantly, who are you trying to kid?

It's Cool Being You

Keeping our identity means keeping a sense of what makes us the person we are. Lose our identity and we've lost ourselves.

By now you should be informed and ready to take on the world. You have a few things to remember, but the main one is to keep true to yourself. Hold on tightly to your identity and don't let it get squashed. Being individual means just that; not conforming to become another uniformed teen who blurs into the crowd. Seen, then instantly forgotten. This

Helen, 32

At school the "in" girls smoked, brought alcohol to the school prom, and had boyfriends. I was the geek. Never even had a boyfriend at school. Recently we had a reunion; I was so nervous, but boy had the tables turned! I'm now a lawyer and live with my fiancé in New York. The "in" crowd girls were still the same: smoking, drinking, screwing around. Except it's not so cool when you hit 30. They mostly still lived in the sleepy town we grew up in; most of them in dead-end jobs. What a pathetic sight, still clinging on to their little clique and the high school mentality they tortured me with.

doesn't mean you have to dye your hair bright orange and wear "look-at-me" makeup. It means keeping your own style. If you like something, wear it; if you don't, ditch it.

Just because your peers think it's cool doesn't mean you have to as well. If everyone did the same thing, wore the same thing, liked the same thing, we'd live in a real boring world. It's people's differences that make them individual. Too often we're led to believe that conforming is the way forward. If no one pushed at the barriers, we wouldn't have the varied and colorful world we live in today. Imagine if pioneers hadn't had the strength to keep asking themselves "I wonder . . ."

not-so-cool school?

School can often be the source of your problems. Some teens cruise through high school, loving every minute. For others it's a time we can't wait to get over and done with. So if school is your idea of hell, you need another road to take when you want some help that your family can't provide. Most neighborhoods have youth clubs, church groups, and community-based social activities. Working with them are youth leaders. Experienced people who have dealt with trillions of teens in trouble. They will be more than happy to offer you advice. If you don't ask—you don't get.

Dreams Can Come True

Every teen has the ability to achieve greatness. It's so true.

Every one of us has it within ourselves to make something great out of our lives. And to achieve we have to let ourselves dream a little and reach for the stars.

Take the word "can't" out of your vocabulary. As soon as you say "I can't," that's a negative response. Replace it with the word "try." You'll try to be a good person, to be true to yourself, your friends and your family. Along the way you'll get some knocks, some will be big, others mere grazes. Each time you have to get up, brush yourself off, and start out again. If you need to be spurred on, ask some adults about their dreams–their answers might surprise you!

Everything in life has the chance to be inspirational . . . and that includes you.

Good luck . . . Oh . . . and stay cool.

Jody x

Help is at Hand

TEEN ISSUES
TeenLine:
24-hour, confidential, state-wide, crisis intervention and referral service for teens.
Tel: 1–800–562–1240 or 1–800–722–4222
www.TheTeenLine.org

National Youth Crisis Hotline:
24-hour hotline that provides referrals for teens.
Tel: 1–800–HIT–HOME (1–800–448–4663)
www.1800hithome.com

SEXUALLY TRANSMITTED DISEASES
National AIDS Hotline.
Tel: 1–800–342–2437
www.ashastd.org/hotlines/index.html#stdaids

National STD Hotline:
Confidential information on the treatment and prevention of STDs.
Tel: 1–800–227–8922
www.ashastd.org/hotlines/index.html#stdaids

SEX AND CONTRACEPTION
Planned Parenthood National Hotline:
24-hour information about contraception and STDs.
Tel: 1–800–230–PLAN (1–800–230–7526)
www.plannedparenthood.org

Not-2-Late:
Directory of doctors, hospitals and family planning clinics that provide emergency contraception.
Tel: 1–888–NOT–2–LATE (1–888–668–2528)
not-2-late.com at http://ec.princeton.edu/

DRUG AND ALCOHOL PROBLEMS
National Drug and Alcohol Treatment Hotline:
Tel: 1–800–662–HELP (1–800–662–4357)

National Drug and Alcohol Treatment Referral Service:
Tel: 1–800–662–HELP
www.samhsa.gov/csat/

PREGNANCY

America's Crisis Pregnancy Hotline:
Confidential information and counseling on pregnancy options
Tel: 1–888–4–OPTIONS
(1–800–467–8466)
www.thehelpline.org

National Campaign to Prevent Teen Pregnancy
www.teenpregnancy.org

National Abortion Federation:
Provides referrals to clinics that perform abortions and answers related questions.
Tel: 1–800–772–9100

GAY AND LESBIAN

The Trevor Helpline:
24-hour, confidential suicide prevention hotline for gay teens.
Tel: 1–800–850–8078

National Gay and Lesbian Hotline:
Counseling services specific to the gay and lesbian community
Tel: 1–888–THE–GLNH
(1–888–843–4564)

SEXUAL AND CHILD ABUSE

National Child Abuse Hotline:
Crisis counseling for sexual abuse, domestic violence, rape, and missing children.
Tel: 1–800–422–4453
www.childhelpusa.org

Rape, Abuse, Incest National Network (RAINN):
24-hour hotline
Tel: 1–800–656–HOPE
(1–800–656–4673)
www.rainn.org

EATING DISORDERS

National Eating Disorders Association:
Counseling for addressing food and body image issues.
Tel: 1–800–931–2237
www.nationaleatingdisorders.org

SUICIDE

Suicide Hotlines:
Tel: 1–800–SUICIDE
(784–2433)
SuicideHotlines.com

Index

A
abuse 65
acid 53
addictions 42–45
adults 37
alcohol 46–49

B
bisexuality 57
boys 58–59, 63
breath test 47
bullying 22–23, 30–39

C
cancer 44
cigarettes 42–45
cliques 20–25
cocaine 52
comforters 28
confidence 48, 68–73
crime 54–55
crushes 57

D
dads 64–65
dares 55
death 34–35
depression 28–31, 33
discrimination 16–17, 36–37
divorce 66–67
drinking 46–49
driving 47, 55
drugs 50–53

E
ecstasy 53
emotions 72–72

F
families 67
fitting in 14–15
friends 12–13, 24–25, 31, 62, 71

G
gangs 55
GHB 53
grieving 35

H
health 43, 49
heroin 52
homoesexuality 57
hormones 28, 57

I, J
individuality 10–11, 14–15, 74–75

K
ketamine 53

L
LSD 53

M
marijuana 51
media pressure 10–11, 18
meth 52
moms 64–65
moods 28–29

N, O
nicotine 43

P, Q
parents 62–65
passion 73
peer pressure 17–19, 36–37, 58–59, 74–75
privacy 63
puberty 57

R
relationships 56–59
rohypnol 53

S
school 25, 63, 75
self control 48–49
self esteem 68–69
sex 49, 56–59
smoking 42–45, 50–51
speaking out 73
stealing 54, 55
step families 66–67
suicide 32–33

T, U, V
teasing 16–17
violence 55

W, X, Y, Z
wine 46
writing 31